To Jo, my English sister, who touched my
life and filled it with colour.

And to all of those who still haven't
found their hidden talents.

G.M.

First published 2013 by Macmillan Children's Books
This edition first published in 2016 by Macmillan Children's Books
an imprint of Pan Macmillan
20 New Wharf Road, London N1 9RR
Associated companies throughout the world
www.panmacmillan.com

ISBN: 978-1-5098-4392-3

1 3 5 7 9 8 6 4 2

A CIP catalogue record for this book is available from the British Library.

Printed in China

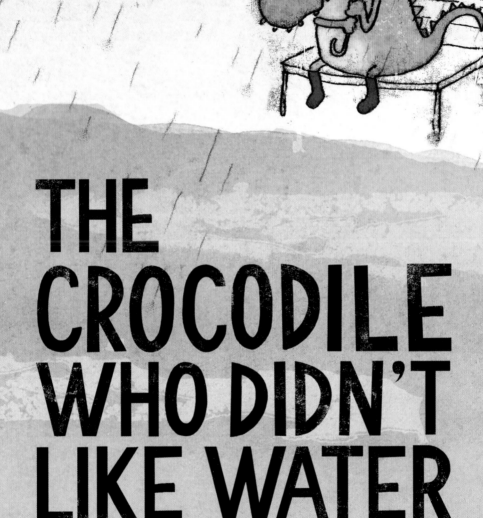

THE CROCODILE WHO DIDN'T LIKE WATER

Gemma Merino

Once upon a time, there
was a little crocodile.

And this little crocodile
didn't like water.

He longed to play with his brothers and sisters.

But they were far too busy with swim club.
And this little crocodile didn't like swim club.

What
he
really
liked
was
climbing
trees!

But nobody else did.

It was lonely having nobody to play with.
So the little crocodile made a decision.

He had saved up his money from the tooth fairy,
and he knew exactly what to buy with it.

The next afternoon he took his
new rubber ring over to the water.
Today he would play with his
brothers and sisters!

But he couldn't play ball.

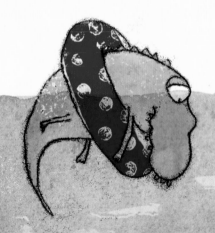

Or swim underwater.

And although climbing the ladder was fun,

he
just
didn't
want
to

J
U
M
P.

But he didn't want to be alone.

So he decided to try, one last time . . .

One,

twooo,

two
and
a
half

THREEEEEE!

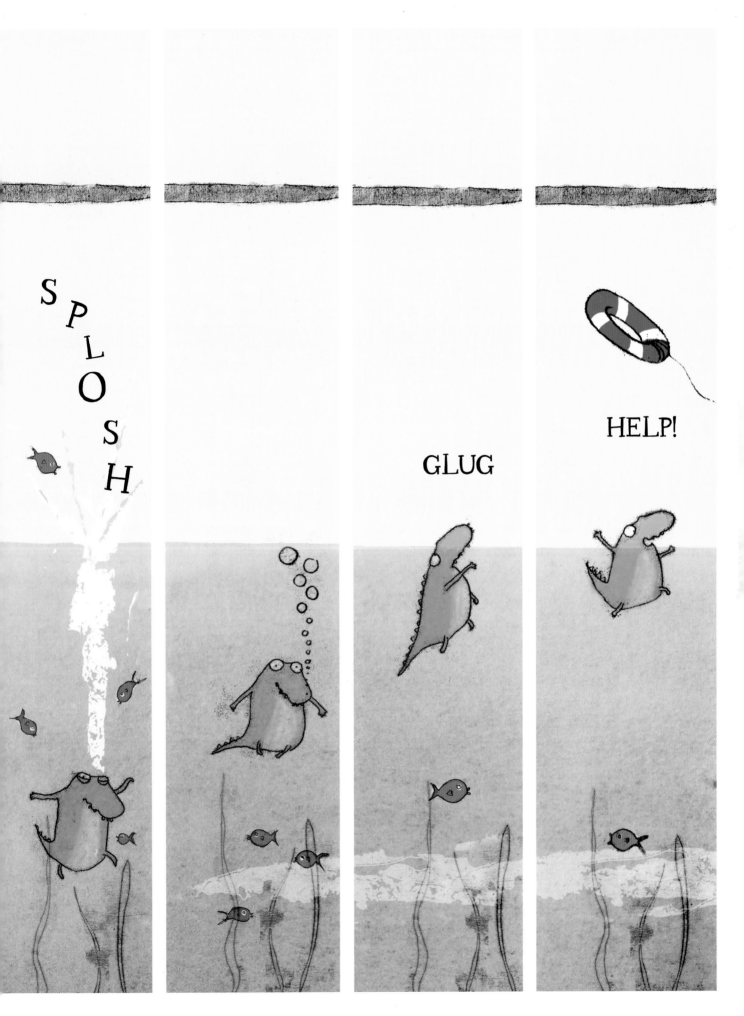

This little crocodile
definitely hated water.
It was cold,
it was wet,
and it was embarrassing.

But then something
strange happened.

His nose began to tickle,

and the tickle grew,

and grew,

and grew,

until . . .

AAAACH

This little crocodile
didn't like water,
because he wasn't
a crocodile at all!

He was a DRAGON.

And this little dragon
wasn't born to swim.

He was born to
breathe fire.

And he was born to fly!